SEA LION ROARS

SMITHSONIAN OCEANIC COLLECTION

To my family and friends on Vancouver Island
and those sea lions swimming offshore
    — D.L.

To my nieces and nephews — Aimee, Colleen, Brian, Julie, and Jeff.
Also to David, Gary, and Eric. Some are grown, all are special.
    — J.S.

Book copyright © 1997 Trudy Corporation, 353 Main Avenue, Norwalk, CT 06851,
and the Smithsonian Institution, Washington, DC 20560.

Soundprints is a division of Trudy Corporation, Norwalk, Connecticut.

Book Design: Shields & Partners, Westport, CT

First Edition 1997
10 9 8 7 6 5 4 3 2
Printed in Singapore

Acknowledgements:
    Our very special thanks to Dr. Charles Handley of the Smithsonian Institution's Department of
Vertebrate Zoology for his curatorial review.
    The author would also like to give her special thanks to Ann Bauer of The Marine Mammal Center,
PIER 39, the New England Aquarium, Chris Read, Dede Rector, and Hugh Ryono.

Library of Congress Cataloging-in-Publication Data

Lamm, C. Drew.

Sea Lion Roars / by C. Drew Lamm; illustrated by Joel Snyder.
       p.   cm.
Summary: On Sea Lion's first birthday, he leaves his rookery in the Channel Islands to make the long journey
to San Francisco Harbor, during which he becomes entangled in a net and must be rescued by workers from the
Marine Mammal Center.
      ISBN 1-56899-400-1
1. Sea lions — Juvenile Fiction. [1. Sea lions — Fiction. 2. Wildlife rescue — Fiction.]
I. Snyder, Joel, ill. II. Title.
      PZ10.3.L33235Se 1997   96-44374
      [Fic] — dc21   CIP
                                        AC

SEA LION ROARS

by C. Drew Lamm   Illustrated by Joel Snyder

Soundprints
Where Children Discover...

Sea Lion wiggles squid tentacles from whisker to whisker. He tosses them — spins, spreads his whiskers — catches them and flings them into the air again. A piece of kelp floats by. Sea Lion twirls, flips backward, catches the kelp, and hurls it into the air. He roars.

This is Sea Lion's first birthday. He's a yearling and he swims like he breathes, smooth and easy!

Sea Lion surfs to his rookery on San Miguel island. On the beach he pushes through the roar of sea lions. He rubs his whiskers over the sand to clean them.

A large male charges down the sand and Sea Lion lopes to the side. He reaches his mother. Mother nudges him away. She has just given birth. She smells her new pup to recognize it among the hundreds of others. They bark back and forth, learning each other's distinct voices.

Soon Mother will swim out to sea to forage for food. But when she returns, she'll find her new pup by its smell and its voice, just as she always found Sea Lion the year before.

Sea Lion sees a rumble of males heading out to the ocean. They porpoise over the waves. Mating season is over. These males want more food and a new place to haul out. Sea Lion leaves home and follows them up the coast of California.

Now it's Sea Lion's baby sister's turn to taste their mother's rich milk. Sea Lion is on his own.

Gulls and petrels fly overhead. A Pacific gray whale glides by. Sea Lion leaps into its wake and rides. He skirts off to the right and dives under the whale. He loops in circles, barking bubbles and chasing them.

Late in the afternoon, he hears a sea lion's alarm bark. He spots a dark shape. Sea Lion shoots toward shore. The sea lions leap ten feet up onto a rock ledge. Below them a great white shark streaks past.

It's hot on the rocks, and Sea Lion sticks a flipper up in the air to cool off.

When all seems still, the sea lions leap off the rocks. They dive, chasing after mackerel and other tasty treats.

Sea Lion dives deep. His whiskers tremble, alert for the vibration of anchovy or squid. He spots a squid, strikes, and feels a tangle of tentacles. Squid slides down his throat.

As night sets, the sea lions close in together. They float as a large "raft." Sea Lion makes sucking sounds with his mouth as he used to do when he nestled with his mother.

As the rising sun glitters across the Pacific Ocean, Sea Lion wakes hungry. Diving, he flies through the water, his flippers like underwater wings. Sea Lion shoots toward a flutter of fins — rockfish caught in an abandoned fishing net. Sea Lion dives, mouth open and....

He feels something loop around his neck. He lashes to the right. The left. He dives. It tightens. He's caught too.

Sea Lion swims and dives until he's limp. The fishing net cuts into him. He swims. But he can't breathe well.

The net pinches his neck.

The other sea lions have gone. For days Sea Lion swims alone, dragging the net behind him. He breathes harder — exhausted. One day he sees above him a golden bridge reaching from one shore to another. Fishing boats hum by. He keeps swimming.

And then, he hears a comforting sound. A bellowing, barking sound. Lolling in a bay are masses of fur, and flippers stuck out in the air like rubber sails.

Beyond them are more sea lions, lumped on floating rocks — docks. Sea Lion hauls out.

A bull snorts and knocks Sea Lion off with a sweep of his head. Sea Lion leaps again. He lands on another snoozing bull. This one moans and rolls over. Sea Lion collapses beside him. Another sea lion lumbers across, looking for space. Sea Lion is squashed as the big male staggers over him.